LACROSSE
FACE-OFF

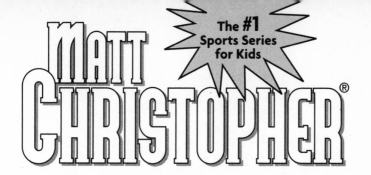

The #1 Sports Series for Kids

LACROSSE
FACE-OFF

Text by Stephanie Peters

LITTLE, BROWN AND COMPANY

New York · Boston

Little, Brown and Company

Time Warner Book Group
1271 Avenue of the Americas, New York, NY 10020
Visit our Web site at www.lb-kids.com

www.mattchristopher.com

First Edition: March 2006

Library of Congress Cataloging-in-Publication Data

Peters, Stephanie True.
    Lacrosse face-off / text written by Stephanie Peters. — 1st ed.
        p. cm.
    "Matt Christopher."
    Summary: Eleven-year-old Garry, embarrassed when his
unathletic brother joins his lacrosse team, faces a bigger problem when the team bully turns on both of them.
    ISBN 0-316-01392-7
    [1. Teamwork (Sports) — Fiction.   2. Bullies — Fiction.
3. Sportsmanship — Fiction.   4. Lacrosse — Fiction.
5. Brothers — Fiction.]   I. Title.

PZ7.P441833La 2005
[Fic] — dc22   2004027841

10   9   8   7   6   5   4   3   2   1

Q-FF

Printed in the United States of America

LACROSSE
FACE-OFF

Eleven-year-old Garry Wallis stood at the edge of the playing field with seventeen other middle-school boys. He gripped his lacrosse stick tightly in one hand. The fingers of his other hand drummed against his leg, the only sign of his nervousness.

Garry had been interested in lacrosse ever since he'd done a school report on the sport in fourth grade. When he'd researched the subject, he'd learned that lacrosse had been invented by Native Americans and was part of the religion of many tribes. They called it "the Creator's game" and featured it in several myths about creation. Long ago, the fast-paced sport was used to train warriors for battle by developing their strength and endurance. Sometimes, instead of actual battles, games were played to settle arguments between warring tribes. And once, lacrosse helped a tribe capture a British fort. The soldiers had become so interested in a match, they hadn't noticed how close the players had come to the fort until it was too late!

The spring after he'd written the report, he'd asked his mother if he could play lacrosse instead of baseball. She'd agreed to let him join the local Lightning Division team. He'd played for that team for the last two years. He loved the game and was pretty good at it too. But this year he was in sixth grade, and that meant he had to move up a level, to the Junior Division. Now he'd be playing with and against sixth- and seventh-graders. One quick glance at his teammates reminded him that many players at this level would be bigger, stronger, and faster.

With a few exceptions, of course, including his older brother, Todd. Todd had never played lacrosse before. He was more of a sit-inside kind of kid than a get-out-and-play sort. His idea of competition was dueling with monster-and-magician trading cards, a game he'd been obsessed with for months. He'd collected such a huge stack of cards that he had to hold them together with a big rubber band.

Garry was pretty sure Todd wouldn't have joined the lacrosse team this year either, if it hadn't been for their last visit to the doctor. Each year Mrs. Wallis brought her sons for their annual checkups. There they were measured and weighed and had their hearts and lungs listened to, their blood pressure taken, and their ears, eyes, and throats examined.

Usually they were declared fit and healthy and sent on their way.

This year, however, the doctor frowned when she looked over Todd's chart. "Todd," she asked, peering over her glasses, "do you exercise regularly?"

Todd shrugged. "I have gym class twice a week at school," he answered.

"Hmmm," the doctor said.

"What is it?" Mrs. Wallis asked anxiously.

"Todd has gained twelve pounds since his last visit," the doctor replied.

"Well, he is a growing boy, after all!" said Mrs. Wallis.

"Er, yes, but the trouble is, he's growing *sideways*, not up. He's only gotten one inch taller in the past year."

Garry snuck a glance at his brother. Now that the doctor mentioned it, Todd *was* looking a little pudgy.

The doctor scribbled something on a piece

of paper as she kept talking. "It is possible that Todd's weight gain is just the beginning of a growth spurt, of course. But what if it isn't? I'm going to give you a prescription that should help. I'd like you to get it filled as soon and as often as possible." She handed the paper to Garry's mother.

Garry looked over her shoulder to see what the doctor had written. There was only one word, but it was underlined three times and had a big exclamation point after it: *Exercise!*

Mrs. Wallis took the doctor's advice seriously. That night, she told Todd to choose some kind of physical activity to do regularly. After much hemming and hawing, he chose lacrosse. "You drag me to all of Garry's games anyway," he said. "I might as well get this exercise stuff over with then."

And so now here they were, the Wallis brothers together on the same lacrosse team.

Garry was pretty sure Todd wasn't the only newcomer to the sport there today. But compared with the other boys, Todd was the least athletic-looking. The protective pads he wore on his arms and shoulders only made him look that much bulkier. Garry wondered if his brother would survive even the first week.

"Hello, boys, and welcome to practice!" A booming voice interrupted Garry's thoughts. He turned to see a man and a boy jogging toward them. Both carried lacrosse sticks and looked so much alike that they were clearly father and son. The father wore a sweatshirt with their team name, "Rockets," across the front. He took out a clipboard, and the son joined Garry and the rest of the team.

"My name is Fred Hasbrouck, but you can call me Coach," the man said. "As some of you know, your old coach retired after last

6

season. I understand that that season was a phenomenal one for this team. First place in the division!" He nodded appreciatively. "Well, many of last year's players have moved up to the next division, but that doesn't mean this team won't be just as strong." He looked at his clipboard. "Now, let's see who you are." He started to read down a list of names.

"Anderson?"

"Here, Coach!"

"Backus?"

"Yo!"

"Donofrio?"

Silence. The coach looked up. "Donofrio?" he repeated.

"Yeah, right here," came a voice from behind the coach.

Garry stared in surprise, then smiled with delight. He hadn't realized that Michael Donofrio was on his team!

Michael was a seventh-grader, like Todd. When Garry had started playing lacrosse in fourth grade, Michael had been on his team. He'd been one of the better players then, and Garry figured he had to be just as good now.

Garry raised a hand in greeting. Michael nodded and moved to the spot next to him. Evan Fitzgerald, the boy who had been standing there, shifted to make room for him.

"Mr. Donofrio, in the future please be on time for practices," the coach said.

Michael shot a finger gun at him. "Gotcha," he said.

Coach Hasbrouck raised an eyebrow, then shook his head slightly and continued down his list. Garry sounded off when his name was called, as did Todd.

Michael stared down the line, then jabbed Garry in the ribs. "Your brother's here too?" he whispered. "Man, I didn't even recognize him! Is it the pads that make him look so

8

fat, or is that he's gotten a little tubby?" He chuckled. "Yeah, that's it, Tubby Todd! Tub-eee Todd. T.T. for short!"

Evan snickered. "Good one, bro," he said. "You crack me up!"

Michael gave Garry a half smile. After a moment, Garry laughed too.

Then Coach Hasbrouck called for their attention, and Garry's first practice as a Junior Division lacrosse player began.

2

The coach started them off with some simple stretches, then had them do push-ups and leg lifts. "The stronger your bodies are, the better the lacrosse players you'll be," he told them. "And because speed and stamina are essential too, let's see you do three laps around the field. Come on, I'll lead the way."

There were some groans, but everyone took off after Coach Hasbrouck. After two laps, Garry was breathing hard. Michael, he noticed, looked as if he could go another three times around without breaking a sweat. He glanced over his shoulder to see how his brother was doing — then quickly turned back. Todd was bringing up the rear and looked like a bear cub lumbering along on two legs.

When the laps were finished, Coach Hasbrouck had them pair off for catching and throwing drills. "Helmets on, everyone, and mouth guards in. Those of you new to lacrosse, try to find a partner who knows what he's doing. Make two lines facing each other about ten yards apart."

"Wallis, you're with me," Michael said. "*Garry* Wallis, that is," he added with a frown when Todd took a step toward him. "I came here to play lacrosse, not babysit a newbie."

Garry saw his brother flush a deep red. He felt a stab of pity for Todd. Then Michael called to him again and the moment passed.

"Okay, listen up and follow my commands,"

Coach Hasbrouck called when everyone was in line. "Ready position!"

Garry snapped his stick up, holding it with the head upright and the shaft angled across the front of his body. One gloved hand gripped the stick beneath the head. The other rested near the end. His feet were shoulder-width apart.

The coach handed out balls to everyone in Michael's line. "I want you to do a top-handed cradle, then throw the ball to your partner, who will do the same. Keep going until I tell you to stop."

Garry bounced on his toes, ready to capture Michael's toss. Michael cradled the ball as instructed, rotating his top hand back and forth to keep the ball in the pocket. His bottom hand held the stick steady so the shaft wouldn't swing around. Then he lobbed the ball in a smooth arc across the field to Garry.

Garry automatically pulled the head back

12

when the ball landed in his pocket, softening the catch so that the ball stuck instead of bouncing out. Judging from the number of balls that fell to the ground, others in his line either forgot to soften or didn't know they were supposed to. Across the field he saw Michael shake his head. Garry concentrated on cradling the ball and throwing an accurate toss to his partner. He breathed a sigh of relief when the ball zoomed directly toward the head of Michael's stick.

Coach Hasbrouck had them continue the drill for fifteen minutes. He made sure they caught the ball three different ways. First he called for stick-side catches — when the ball came to the head of the stick without the players having to move it much. Then he had them catch on their off-stick sides. This was a little more difficult because the catcher had to sweep the stick across his face to make the catch.

Last, the coach had them try over-the-shoulder catches. Those without the ball turned their backs to their partners and held their sticks in ready position. When the partners threw, each receiver looked over his shoulder, twisted the stick so the pocket faced the ball, and caught it without turning around. The trick was realizing which side the ball was going to, the right or the left, and making sure the stick was over that same shoulder.

Garry dropped a fair share of over-the-shoulder catches, but not as many as some of his teammates. Michael, on the other hand, mishandled only a few. It was obvious to Garry that Michael was a very good player, maybe even the best on the team. The fact that he had chosen Garry for his partner made Garry feel good.

The coach called for a two-minute water break, then told them to find new partners for the next drill. This time Garry was paired up with the coach's son.

"Hi, my name's Jeff," the boy said, holding out a gloved hand. "I just moved to town a month ago."

Garry shook it. "I'm Garry, Garry Wallis," he replied.

"Oh, Todd's brother, right?" Jeff said. "I was with him on the last drill. He's new to lacrosse, isn't he?"

Garry looked at Jeff quickly, unsure if the boy was taking a jab at his brother's lack of skill. But he simply seemed to be making an observation. "Uh, yeah, except for throwing the ball around with me in the backyard a few times, he's hardly ever held a stick before," Garry finally said.

Jeff shrugged. "Well, if he's worried he won't see any playing time, tell him not to be. My dad's big on making sure everyone gets into every game."

They stopped talking to listen to the coach explain the drill. "We're going to work on cradling the ball while running. One player will be the ball handler. The other will try to get him to drop the ball by chasing him around the square." He indicated areas he had marked off with orange cones. "There is to be no, I repeat, *no* contact between the two players. Ball handlers, focus on cradling and keeping your body between the ball and your opponent. Chasers, do your best to make him fumble the ball. The goal is to hang on to the ball for ten seconds."

There were four squares, so four pairs of boys took their turns while the rest of the team watched. Garry and Jeff were in the first group. Jeff had the ball. When the coach blew his whistle, Jeff started moving around the square. Garry went after him, but Jeff was quick. He dodged, feinted, and twisted away from Garry, all the while cradling the ball in the pocket. After ten seconds, Garry hadn't come close to forcing him to drop it.

The coach blew his whistle, and the ball handlers became the chasers. When the ten seconds had passed, Garry was panting — but he still had the ball. He and Jeff stepped out of the square to let the next pair have their turn.

Jeff grinned at him. "I'd say we're pretty evenly matched, wouldn't you?"

Garry nodded. "What position do you usually play?"

"I've played everything except goalkeeper," Jeff replied, "but I like middie best."

"Yeah, I wouldn't mind playing midfield," Garry agreed. "But I like attack position better."

"You like to score, huh?"

"Well, as my mother might say, it's right up there with winning the lottery!" Garry quipped.

Jeff threw his head back and laughed. Garry laughed too.

Jeff's a good kid, he thought. *I bet he's lonely, being new and all.* He decided to invite him over to hang out after practice. He opened his mouth to ask when suddenly he heard a sharp cry. He turned to see what the problem was — and his eyes widened with horror.

3

Todd lay on the ground, clutching his ankle. The coach was kneeling beside him. Michael stood off to the side.

Jeff turned to Evan. "What happened?"

"I'm not sure," Evan answered. "One minute Michael and Todd were doing the drill, the next Todd was eating dirt."

Coach Hasbrouck beckoned to Garry. Garry hurried onto the field, hooked an arm under his brother, and helped hoist him to his feet. With Todd between them, the coach and Garry guided Todd to a bench. Michael followed.

"He must have tripped over something, Coach," Michael said.

Todd's head snapped up. "Yeah," he said angrily. "Your stick!"

Michael's jaw dropped. "You're accusing me of tripping you?" he asked, his voice filled with disbelief. He turned to Coach Hasbrouck. "I swear, I wasn't even anywhere near him when he went down!"

"He wasn't, Coach," Evan suddenly piped up. "I saw the whole thing. Todd just fell."

Garry stared at him in surprise. "But didn't you just tell Jeff that —"

"— that Todd was just starting to get the hang of cradling when he tripped?" Michael cut in. He laid a hand on Todd's shoulder. "I was going to say the same thing. Really, T.T., for a newbie, you were doing great."

Todd blinked. "Uh, thanks, Michael," he said after a moment. He sounded confused.

Coach Hasbrouck stood up. "Todd, take a

few minutes. The rest of you, resume the drill. And let's all be careful out there, okay?"

Garry and Jeff trotted back to a square. "Am I mistaken," Jeff said in a low voice, "or did Evan just lie for Michael?"

Garry scuffed his foot in the grass. He wasn't sure what to make of the exchange either. The fact that Michael had called Todd "T.T." hadn't escaped him, but then again Michael had also given Todd a compliment.

"I don't know," he said at last. "To be perfectly honest, I wouldn't be surprised if my brother *did* trip over his own feet. He's not the most athletic kid around, in case you hadn't noticed."

Jeff gave him a funny look. "He's not that bad. And you've got to admit it's weird. One minute Evan says he doesn't know what happened, the next he's claiming that he saw the whole thing. Has he got something against your brother?"

Garry glanced over at Todd. His brother's leg was stretched out on the bench, an ice pack on his ankle. Todd's head and arms hung over the back of the bench, making his round stomach appear even rounder. Garry looked away. "Let's just forget about Todd and get back to practice."

The team continued to do the cradling drill. Todd rejoined them after five minutes, still limping slightly. Twenty minutes later, the coach announced that practice was through for the day. Garry was tired, but his brother looked completely done in.

And at home later that night, Todd fell asleep on the couch. Garry picked up the book his brother had been reading, marked the page for him, then tiptoed away.

For the second time that day, he wondered if his brother would make it through the first week of practice. It seemed doubtful. *After all,* he thought, *he almost didn't make it through the first day!*

Todd did make it through the week, but just barely. He always brought up the rear in the warm-up laps, collapsed after push-ups, and turned beet red with exertion when doing leg lifts. He was clearly the worst player on the team. The only person who regularly chose him for a drill partner was Jeff.

Garry, meanwhile, found himself paired with Michael most often — much to Evan's chagrin, he noticed. In fact, Evan reminded Garry of a cartoon he'd seen once in which a small puppy followed a bulldog everywhere, doing everything the bulldog asked him to do, no matter how absurd the request. In Garry's mind, Evan was that puppy, willing and eager to do anything Michael asked of him.

Well, Garry wasn't about to take Evan's

place as Michael's puppy, but he had to admit he liked working out with the best player on the team. Who wouldn't?

Early in the week, Coach Hasbrouck had announced that the team would host a car wash that Saturday to raise money for their annual dues to the league. Michael had raised his hand and asked why they couldn't just ask their parents to pay the dues for them. Mr. Hasbrouck had replied that he preferred for the money to come from a team effort. "If we all work together, we'll have no problem earning what we need," he'd said.

After practice on Friday the coach reminded them to be in the school parking lot bright and early on Saturday morning. He asked everyone to bring a bucket and a rag or sponge. Jeff volunteered to make signs. Todd immediately said he'd help him. So instead of going home with Garry that night, Todd went with the Hasbroucks.

As Garry watched his brother walk to the parking lot with Jeff and the coach, he felt a spark of jealousy. Todd had pulled out his stack of monster-and-magician cards and was showing them to Jeff. Jeff was nodding enthusiastically.

Then Garry shrugged. *Jeff is probably just lonely, being new in town and all,* he told himself again as he climbed into his mother's car. *Or maybe Jeff feels sorry for Todd. I know I do, the way he lumbers around the field, trips over his feet, and misses practically every ball thrown to him. But what can you do? You can't make someone into a lacrosse player overnight!*

4

The next morning was warm and sunny, perfect weather for a car wash. Garry changed out of his pajamas and into a bathing suit and T-shirt and headed down the stairs for breakfast. Todd was already at the table. Three trading cards were spread out in front of him.

"New cards?" Garry asked.

Todd nodded. "Jeff and I traded last night after we finished the signs. He's got a whole stack too." He gathered up the cards, secured them with the rubber band, and glanced at his watch. "You better eat something quick, or we'll be late for the car wash."

Garry grabbed two doughnuts out of a box, crammed one into his mouth, chewed and swallowed, then ate the other one in two bites. He washed it all down with a glass of juice.

"Ready!" he said, his mouth ringed with powdered sugar.

Mrs. Wallis drove them to the school. They collected their buckets and sponges from the trunk and hurried to join their teammates. Jeff waved to them as they approached.

"Don't the signs look great?" he called. "It was Todd's idea to do them on black poster paper and outline the neon green paint with glitter, so the words would stand out more. You can see them a mile away!"

Garry had to admit that the signs looked

good, and he told his brother as much. Then the car wash began.

Mr. Hasbrouck had organized the perfect washing system. Cars drove to a spot where a boy waited with a hose. When the car was completely wet, two other boys slopped sudsy water onto every inch of the vehicle. Another scrubbed the tires, and a fifth polished the mirrors and fenders. Then the first boy hosed it clean, and it was the next car's turn.

Garry, Jeff, Todd, and two other boys worked as one team, while the other boys broke into three more groups of five. By noontime, the four car-washing squads had cleaned nearly fifty cars and earned enough money for the league dues.

"I'm starving!" Jeff announced, throwing his worn-out sponge into an empty bucket. "Dad, didn't you bring a bunch of sandwiches and chips?"

"Sure did." He gestured to a large cooler resting on the grass. "There should be enough sandwiches for everyone to get one. Drinks too."

The boys cheered, and Jeff and Todd set about distributing the food. Garry had just popped the last bite of his peanut-butter-and-jelly into his mouth when a blast of cold water struck him in the back.

"Hey!" he cried. He turned to find Michael grinning and pointing a hose at him. Garry grinned back, jumped to his feet, and tackled the older boy. They wrestled for a minute, then Garry freed the hose from Michael's grasp. "Now you're going to get it!" he bellowed.

He cranked the nozzle on. Nothing happened. Puzzled, he turned the nozzle toward himself, trying to see what was wrong. Suddenly, water shot out and hit him directly in the face. With a yelp, he dropped the hose. When his vision cleared he saw Evan bent over laughing, one hand on the spigot.

He also saw Todd and Jeff sneaking up behind Evan with a bucket of sudsy water. Two seconds later, the bucket was empty, Evan was soaking wet, and Todd, Jeff, and everyone else on the team were the ones doubled over with laughter.

"Hey, that's not funny!" Evan's face was purple with anger.

Coach Hasbrouck handed him a dry towel. "Oh, come on now, Evan, it's just a little soap and water," he chided. "You know, good *clean* fun!"

Evan gave Todd and Jeff one last dirty look, then stalked away to sulk.

The rest of the boys gathered up the sponges, towels, soap, and buckets. Then the coach called them together. "Okay, boys, good work today. I hope to see the same kind of teamwork next week. I've arranged for us to play a scrimmage on Friday against the Panthers." The team buzzed with excitement. "Practices will focus on game situations for most of next week. That means plenty of running, boys, so be sure to get your rest this weekend."

5

Monday afternoon, Coach Hasbrouck put the team through ten minutes of warm-ups. After the laps were done, he worked on stick skills, then moved on to checking drills.

"Those of you new to the Junior Division will face body checking for the first time this season," he reminded them. "The referees will be watching you carefully to be sure you're doing this move correctly and legally."

He motioned for Jeff to step forward. "Body checking is legal only when done to the ball carrier or to an opponent who is within five yards of the ball. Contact is made below the shoulder and above the knees, to the front or side of the body." He indicated the legal checking areas on Jeff's body. "Like a tackle in football, you run at your opponent and drive into him with your shoulder and upper body." He demonstrated the move on Jeff in slow motion.

"Use your heads when bodychecking. Or rather," he corrected with a grin, "*don't* use your heads. Helmets or no, checking with your head will hurt."

Everyone laughed until the coach held up a gloved hand. "Lacrosse is an aggressive game, so be prepared to check and be checked. But be warned: if you illegally bodycheck an opponent, the ref will give you a one-, two-, or even three-minute penalty. Three minutes is a long time to run a team short sided, folks. The other team can score a whole lot of goals if they have one less player to worry about."

Coach Hasbrouck instructed them to pair off and practice body checks. Garry looked to see if Michael wanted to partner up, but Evan had already claimed him. So instead Garry practiced the move with another sixth-grader, a stocky but surprisingly quick boy named Christopher. They knocked each other back and forth for ten minutes, trading places as ball carrier and checker.

Finally, the coach called everyone together and told them it was time to scrimmage. He divided the team into two squads of ten and assigned each player a position.

Garry was an attacker, along with Michael and a sixth-grader named Carl. Carl looked nervous until Michael slung an arm around his shoulders and said, "Don't worry, kid, just feed me the ball and I'll take care of everything." Michael pointed a finger gun at Garry and added, "Same goes for you, Wallis. The name of the game is put-the-ball-in-the-net, and I'm the one who does that best!"

Behind the attackers were three midfielders, seventh-grade boys Garry was still getting to know. Behind them were the three defenders. Todd was with this group, on the left. Jeff was in goal.

Coach Hasbrouck called the two center attackers together for the face-off. Michael and his opponent lowered their sticks to the ground and crouched down over them, their helmets nearly touching. The coach put the ball between the centers, took a step back, and blew his whistle.

Michael exploded into action. He flipped his stick over, clamped the ball, and raked it away from his opponent in one smooth motion. Carl ran in and scooped up the loose ball. He immediately passed it to Michael, who sprinted downfield toward the opposite goal. Garry hustled after him, ready to help out as needed.

But Michael didn't need help. Cradling the ball in the pocket, he cut left, dodged around a midfielder, and used his body as a shield when a second player tried to stick-check the ball loose. Suddenly, he was in the attack area to the right of the goal. He slashed his stick downward and threw. The hard white sphere hurtled past the goalie and swished into the net.

"Yes!" Michael cried, pumping his gloved fist above his head. He pretended to lick his finger and chalked up a tally mark in the air. Then it was back to center field for another face-off.

Once again Michael pulled the ball away from his opponent, but this time it was the other team that captured it. The right attacker threw it to his center, a sixth-grader named Conor. Conor started to run downfield, but

Michael bodychecked him before he had gone two steps. The bump came as a surprise to the attacker, and he stumbled. The ball popped free. Michael was about to scoop it up when Coach Hasbrouck blew his whistle to stop the play.

"Okay, boys, let's try to keep the body checks to a minimum for this scrimmage," he called. "I don't want anyone getting hurt before our first game. Focus on your passes and on working the ball around the field instead." The coach tossed the ball to Conor and jogged to the sideline. His back was turned, so he didn't see Michael roll his eyes in disgust.

But practically everyone else on the team saw it. And Garry was close enough to hear Michael mutter, "Just what I always wanted: a team of wusses, coached by the head wuss himself."

6

For the rest of the week, the coach followed a similar format for practices — warm-ups followed by drills, and then scrimmages. Midway through Wednesday's practice, he showed them the proper technique for a poke check, holding his stick parallel to the ground and jabbing his opponent's stick to make him drop the ball.

"And remember," he added, "the ball carrier's gloved hand is considered part of the stick, so it's legal to poke-check that hand. Anything else, however, is off-limits. You'll be called for slashing, a one-minute penalty.

Also, if you use the shaft of the stick to check, you'll be called for cross-checking, which earns you, you guessed it, a one-minute penalty. So just use the head with the poke check, all right?"

During scrimmages, the coach mixed up the teams often, trying different players out in different positions. After Thursday's practice, he called everyone together to announce the starting lineup for the next day's scrimmage against the Panthers.

"Attackers will be Garry, Michael, and Conor."

Garry and Conor exchanged high fives. Garry turned to do the same with Michael, but Michael just grimaced and said, "Dude, back off. My starting position was a given."

"Evan, Jeff, and Samuel will be at midfield," the coach continued. "At defense, let's have Carl, Eric, and Brandon. Christopher will be in goal."

Then he passed out the team uniforms. "Brand-new this year," he said, handing Garry a jersey with the number 33 on it. The shirt was reversible — white on one side for home games, bright yellow on the other for when the team played away games. The team name, "Rockets," was in bold black lettering on both sides.

As Garry put his jersey into his equipment bag, he heard someone stifle a snicker.

"No way that shirt'll fit over his gut *and* his pads!"

Garry jerked his head up. He saw Todd holding his jersey up against his body — and Evan and Michael laughing together.

Todd must have heard them too. He balled up the jersey and shoved it into his duffel bag, a dull red flush creeping up his neck.

Garry looked away, feeling embarrassed for his brother and wishing again that Todd were in better shape. Out of the corner of his eye, he noticed Jeff pull Todd aside and start talking to him in a low voice. Todd's face cleared. He nodded a few times, said "be right back," and headed toward Garry.

Garry quickly busied himself with zipping his bag, trying to act as if he hadn't heard and seen everything.

"Could you tell Mom I'm going to Jeff's house?" Todd said when he reached him. "Coach Hasbrouck will drive me home before dinner."

"Uh, sure, Todd," Garry said, still not facing his brother. He could feel Todd staring at him, though, and he was about to return the look when Michael called to him.

"Hey, Wallis, Evan and me are heading to the candy store. Want to come?"

"Let me check with my mom," he called back. He finally looked at his brother, but the hurt he saw in Todd's eyes was so strong

41

that he quickly lowered his gaze. "I guess I'll see you at home later."

"Whatever." Todd spun on his heel and headed toward Jeff. Garry picked up his equipment bag and walked to where Michael and Evan were horsing around. For some reason, he felt as if he was joining the enemy.

The next morning, Garry entered the kitchen determined to make amends with his brother.

"Hey, Todd," he said during breakfast, "want to walk to school together?"

Todd gave him a suspicious look. Usually Garry ran ahead to school, complaining that his brother walked too slowly.

"Come on, what do you say?" Garry wheedled.

Todd agreed reluctantly. They shouldered their backpacks and picked up their equipment bags and lacrosse sticks from the garage. The silence as they walked was so stony that after five minutes Garry felt like screaming, just to hear a noise. Instead, he asked Todd what he and Jeff had done after practice the day before.

"You guys trade some more cards or something?"

"No," came Todd's short reply.

"Oh." More silence. He tried again. "Hey, you want some gum? I got some yesterday when I was at the candy store with . . . um, when I was at the candy store." He dug a piece out of his pocket with his free hand. "Here, it's sugarless."

Todd stared at the gum. Then he gave a small smile, shifted his lacrosse stick to his other side, and reached toward his brother's outstretched hand. As he did, something green whizzed past him and struck his arm.

"Ow!" Todd cried, dropping his lacrosse stick and equipment bag so he could clutch the injured spot. "What was that?"

Garry had already found the object that had hit his brother. With his lacrosse stick, he reached over and scooped up a green Super Ball.

"Whose is that?" Todd asked.

"It's Evan's. He bought it at the candy store yesterday."

Todd glanced around nervously.

Garry tossed the ball up and caught it with his stick. "Evan, come out or I'm chucking this thing so far you'll never find it."

"You do and you'll be sorry." Evan jumped down from the tree where he'd been hiding. "Give it here," he demanded.

Garry quickly lifted the head of his stick high above his head. "Promise you won't throw this at anyone else and I'll let you have it," he said.

Evan glared at him, then up at the ball. "I promise," he sneered after a moment.

"Good. Now I'll let you have it," Garry responded. He swung the stick down and smacked Evan in the arm just hard enough to sting. The ball popped out and bounced into the grass.

Todd's eyes grew big. He moved a few steps away.

"Hey!" Evan said, rubbing his arm. "What'd you do that for?"

"Told you I'd let you have it, didn't I?" Garry chuckled. "Now you and Todd are even, bruise for bruise."

Evan picked up his ball. "I oughta teach you a lesson, Wallis," he said menacingly.

Garry stuck his nose in Evan's face. "You'd be stupid if you tried. It's two against one."

Evan stepped back. His eyes shifted to Garry's right. A slow smile crossed his face. "Actually, I'd say the odds are all even." He

45

jerked his chin at something behind Garry and started to laugh.

Garry looked over his shoulder just in time to see his brother disappear over the next hill.

7

Garry was still fuming when he arrived at the lacrosse field that afternoon. *I can't believe my own brother ditched me,* he thought for the hundredth time that day. He also couldn't believe he'd been able to talk Evan out of beating him up.

"You owe me one, Wallis," Evan had finally said before sauntering off in the direction of the school. Garry had waited until he was out of sight before picking up his gear and following. He'd been a few minutes late for school but figured that tardiness was better than walking anywhere near Evan when he was angry.

He planned to avoid the older boy before the game as well, but to his surprise Evan seemed to have forgotten the whole incident by that afternoon.

"Yo, Wallis," he said, slinging an arm around Garry's shoulders, "you got your game face on?"

"Oh, uh, you bet!" Garry replied, slightly taken aback by the boy's friendliness.

"Great! I'll be right behind you every step of the way!"

Garry shrugged out from beneath Evan's arm. He turned to reach into his equipment bag for his mouth guard. He caught Todd staring at him. Anger at his brother washed over him again.

"What are you looking at?" he growled. Todd blinked and dropped his gaze.

The coach called them together before

the scrimmage to go over the starting lineup again. Then he put the clipboard aside. "By the way, don't get too comfortable in those positions, starters. I'll be using this scrimmage to try different players out in different positions. Those of you who are used to playing attack may find yourself in goal — and vice versa. And everybody will see playing time today, and in regular games as well. Now do some stretches and get ready to play some good lax."

The scrimmage with the Panthers started ten minutes later. A handful of fans filled the stands, including Garry and Todd's mother. Garry gave her a small wave, then hurried out to the restraining box, where he'd wait during the face-off.

Michael strode to the center. He gave Garry a thumbs-up sign. Then he pointed a finger at him, thumped his own chest, and pointed at the goal. His message was clear:

You get me the ball. I'll score the goals. He gave Conor the same signals.

The referee jogged to the midfield mark. Michael and the Panthers center crouched down. Garry's heart started beating fast with anticipation. He bounced on his toes, ready to move. The ref placed the ball between the two centers, stepped back, and blew his whistle.

Quick as lightning, Michael flipped his stick over to clamp the ball. At the same time, he turned a quarter step over the center line so his body was facing the sideline. Garry couldn't make out what was happening because Michael's back was between him and the ball. Then suddenly the ref signaled that the Rockets had possession, and the ball shot out across the grass toward Garry. Garry dove for it, scooped it up, and started running, cradling the ball safely in the pocket of his stick.

A Panther middie rushed him, stick outstretched in classic poke-check position. Garry didn't give him a chance to try the maneuver, however. He spun away, using his right shoulder as a block. As he twisted around he looked over his left shoulder for someone to pass to. Michael raised his stick in the air, signaling that he was ready. Garry came out of the spin and threw a hard pass.

Michael caught the ball and dashed downfield. Garry, Conor, and two Rockets middies kept pace.

"Go, Michael, go!" Evan screamed from behind them.

A defenseman came toward Michael. Michael switched from a two-handed to a one-handed cradle. He used his free arm to shield his stick. As the defenseman lowered his shoulder for a body check, Michael took a quick step to one side. The Panther followed — only to find empty space. Michael had executed a perfect inside-and-out dodge, luring the defenseman one way with that first step, then switching directions. By the time the Panther realized what had happened, Michael was six steps closer to the goal and in prime scoring position. With a quick flick, he hurled the ball into the upper left corner of the net. *Swish!* Goal!

Michael slow-jogged in a semicircle back to the center, arms held wide and a triumphant grin on his face. "Thank you, thank you!" he called, bowing his head again and again. Evan applauded long and loud.

Garry trotted back to his starting position, wondering why he was suddenly thinking of a film he'd once seen of a prince riding on his horse through a crowd of bowing subjects.

Michael won the face-off again, but this time a Panther swooped in and took possession of the ball before Conor or Garry could get to it. As the Panther rushed into Rockets territory, Garry, Michael, and Conor slowed to a stop. Each had played lacrosse long enough to know that the defending team had to keep three players on their opponent's side when the ball was near their own goal. Otherwise, they'd be called offsides and earn a thirty-second penalty.

Luckily, the ball didn't stay near the Rockets goal for long. Jeff poke-checked the Panther's bottom glove and the Panther dropped the ball. Eric, a Rockets defense-man, scooped it up and cleared it to Evan, who was waiting near the sideline. Evan made a clean catch. Garry, Conor, and Michael were already heading toward the Panthers goal.

For a moment, Garry thought they had a fast break. But the Panthers middies were on them too quickly, and they were forced to slow down. Evan passed the ball to Conor.

"Feed it to me! Feed it to me!" Michael yelled from a spot near the goal. But he was so well covered that Garry could see there was no way for Conor to get a pass through to him. Conor must have figured that too, because after a split-second hesitation, he threw to Garry.

Garry caught the ball close to the sideline. He had a space of open field in front of him and took off at a dead run. A middie sprinted toward him to cut him off. Garry turned his body slightly to protect his stick. The Panther edged up close and started nudging Garry with his arm. Garry pushed back, still running.

He's trying to get me out of bounds! Garry realized. He knew that if the Panther succeeded, the Rockets would lose possession of the ball. That's when he saw Jeff running toward him. Garry slashed his stick downward, being careful not to connect with the Panther, and passed the ball to Jeff.

Jeff bobbled the catch, and the ball bounced away from him. He tore after it. So did Michael and two Panthers. All four sticks stabbed at the ball as each player fought to gain possession. Garry danced from foot to foot, ready to move where needed.

Jeff came away with the ball and instantly threw it to Garry. But the throw was wild, and the ball sailed over the sideline. The ref blew his whistle and awarded possession to the Panthers. A Panther midfielder retrieved the ball, stepped back onto the field, and play resumed.

This time, it ended with a Panthers goal. Christopher, the Rockets goalie, swept his stick through the grass, clearly disgusted with himself. As Garry returned to the midfield line for the face-off, he couldn't help noticing the deep scowl on Michael's face.

"Hey, it's just one goal," he called to the center. "We'll still get 'em!"

"We better," Michael snarled, "because if this is a loser team, we're going to have to make some changes."

8

Garry didn't have time to wonder what Michael meant by "changes." The ref placed the ball between Michael and the Panthers center, and the battle for the ball began again.

Seven minutes and a great deal of running, passing, throwing, and scoring later, the first ten-minute quarter ended. The score was 5–4 in favor of the Rockets. Michael had scored all but one of the goals for their team. As he walked to the bench, he accepted congratulations from his teammates. Evan praised him the loudest, giving a play-by-play of each goal between gulps of water.

"Man, you *killed* their defenseman when you did that pick-and-roll right at the top of the crease! Then it was *zoom* and into the net. Totally sweet."

Garry was pleased they were winning too, but if being ahead meant listening to Evan kiss up to Michael, he almost wished they were losing.

During the break, Coach Hasbrouck announced some substitutions. "Garry, you and Conor stay in. Michael, come on out for a well-deserved rest. Evan, move up to his position. Andrew, take Evan's place at midfield. Christopher, I'm going to keep you in goal for now, but let's see Todd go in for Carl, and Pedro in for Eric. The rest of you, stay in your positions but be on the lookout for subs on the fly."

Garry snuck a look at Michael. The coach had said he wanted Michael on the bench for a "well-deserved rest," but Garry could tell that Michael resented being taken out of the game. Michael pulled Evan aside and whispered intently in his ear. Evan chewed his bottom lip and nodded. Then the ref whistled for the second quarter to begin, and the Rockets hurried onto the field.

"Okay, people, let's take these guys for everything!" Evan cried. Although his words were meant to show strength, Garry thought the older boy sounded nervous.

This should be interesting, he thought. He wondered what Michael had said to him.

"Go, Todd! Go, Garry!"

The sound of his mother's voice reminded Garry that Todd was now in the game. He looked back to see how his brother was doing. He couldn't see his face behind the mask, but the way he was shifting from foot to foot told Garry that his brother was either as nervous as Evan or else so ready to play that he couldn't stand still.

Garry prayed it was the latter but feared the worst. After all, how good could his brother be after less than two weeks of playing a sport that most of the other players — including the competition — had all been playing for years?

He got an answer to that question soon after the face-off. Evan fought hard for the ball, but it was the Panthers that gained possession.

"Fast break!" Garry heard the Panthers ball carrier yell.

A second Panthers attacker cut to the center of the field, leaving Samuel three steps behind him. The ball carrier threw the ball, and the attacker caught it at a dead run. Garry thought the new ball carrier would head for the goal, but instead he dished the ball back to the first Panther, who had run up alongside him in anticipation of the pass. Now they were within attack range, with only Christopher and the defensemen to deal with. One of those defensemen was Todd.

"Bodycheck him! Bodycheck him!" Garry muttered through clenched teeth. As if he'd heard his brother, Todd put his shoulder down and charged the ball carrier.

Unfortunately, Pedro had the same idea. He reached the Panther a split second before Todd did. Pedro's shoulder connected with the Panther's midsection — and Todd's shoulder connected with Pedro's back. The three boys tumbled to the ground, the ball bounced out of bounds behind the goal, and the ref rushed forward, blowing his whistle and waving his arms to stop the clock.

The boys slowly untangled themselves and stood up. Garry could hear his brother apologizing to Pedro, but Pedro just waved him off. Possession was awarded to the Panthers since one of their players was closest to the place where the ball went out of bounds. Moments later, they scored to tie the game.

"Wallis, you're out!" Garry heard someone yell as he jogged back to the midfield. He shook his head. He felt sorry for his brother for seeing so little game time. But he understood why the coach was sending a sub in for him. He'd do the same thing in Coach Hasbrouck's place.

"Garry, what are you, deaf? Didn't you hear me tell you you're out?"

Garry spun around in surprise. Carl was gesturing wildly for him to get off the field.

"*Me?*" Garry asked even as he backpedaled over the sideline. Carl just ignored him and got into position for the face-off.

As he approached the team bench, Garry looked to see who else was sitting there. When he didn't see his brother, he realized that Todd must still be in the game. He turned his attention back to the field — and sucked in his breath. Todd *was* on the field, but he wasn't playing defense anymore. He was on the front line with Carl and Jeff. Evan was on defense.

Michael, however, was still out of the game. Garry took one look at the seventh-grader's dark scowl and hurried to a spot at the opposite end of the bench.

9

Play started up again. Carl managed to clamp the ball during the face-off, but when he tried to send it to a teammate it rolled free and a Panther scooped it up.

The Panthers quickly penetrated past the Rockets midfielders. Then an attacker bobbled the ball. Evan scooped it up right from in front of the Rockets goal and cleared it out to Jeff, who was dancing along the sideline.

It was a soft throw. Jeff had to lunge with his stick outstretched, pocket skyward, to make the catch. Once he had the ball, he swung the stick, head up high, and made a beeline for the opposite end of the field. As he ran he moved his stick to his right hand, twisting it in a perfect one-handed cradle, and held off a Panther with the other. A few steps later he stopped short, put his free hand on the stick, and jerked a quick pass to Todd.

Garry squeezed his eyes shut. When he opened them again, he was amazed to see that his brother had made the catch and was running toward the goal. Unfortunately, Todd must have forgotten to cradle the ball. After a few steps the ball flew out of the pocket and bounced onto the field toward a Panthers midfielder's feet.

The Panther scooped it up and hurled it to where his teammate waited at the sideline. Three quick passes and one shot on goal later, the Panthers had added another point to their side of the scoreboard.

Garry clenched his teeth to keep himself from yelling. Michael threw up his hands and shook his head, plainly disgusted. Others on the bench grumbled and shifted in their seats.

As Todd, Carl, and Jeff returned to the midfield for the face-off, Coach Hasbrouck called for a time-out. Then he gestured for Todd to come to the sideline.

"At last," Garry heard Michael mutter. The older boy stood up, grabbed his stick, and prepared to run onto the field at the coach's signal.

But Coach Hasbrouck didn't pull Todd from the game. Instead, he spoke to the boy while demonstrating something with Todd's stick. Todd frowned at first, then nodded his understanding.

What is going on? Garry wondered. He found out a moment later. When the ref blew his whistle to restart play, Todd rushed onto the field — and right to the center, for the face-off.

Michael sagged back onto the bench. "You have *got* to be kidding me," he said.

Garry didn't say anything, but inside he was thinking the same thing. *Todd, taking the face-off? Is the coach out of his mind?*

It came as no surprise to Garry that Todd didn't win the stick war. What did surprise him was what Todd did next. As the Panthers attacker sent the ball to his teammate, Todd lowered a shoulder and bodychecked him. Unfortunately, by the time he hit the Panther, the attacker no longer had the ball. And Todd's shoulder struck him in the small of the back.

The whistle shrieked. "One-minute penalty, illegal checking!" the ref yelled, pointing at Todd. Todd looked to the coach, clearly unsure of what to do. The coach motioned for him to step off the field into the penalty box. Once Todd crossed the sideline, play resumed.

Since the Rockets were down a player, the Panthers had a big advantage. They used it well, sending the ball past the middies and jockeying for position near the goal. The Rockets defense did the best they could to stay on top of their opponents, but the Panthers were just too quick. The ball carrier slashed his stick downward and the ball flew into the net.

"Oh, come *on!*" Michael yelled. He stood up and paced behind the bench. When Todd went back onto the field to take another face-off, Michael smacked his fist so hard against the bench that Garry could feel the vibrations at the other end.

Man, am I glad it's not me *he's mad at!* he was thinking, when suddenly a heavy hand grabbed his shoulder and twisted him around.

"You and me, we're going to have a little talk after the game," Michael growled. "Behind the bleachers. Be there — or else."

10

Garry, Michael, and two other Rockets went back into the game shortly before the half-time break. Garry played well and even managed to score a few goals.

But it was Michael who took control of the game. He threw with such force that Garry could hear the mesh of his pocket sing. He pushed past, dodged around, and spun away from Panthers players as if his life depended upon it. A few times he bodychecked an opponent so hard that the other player was knocked backward. Nothing he did was illegal — it was just much more aggressive than Garry was used to.

Garry suspected that the Panthers weren't used to such play either. He almost felt sorry for them. The more forceful Michael became, the farther they stayed away from him. By the end of the third quarter, Michael was scoring nearly every time he had the ball. When Coach Hasbrouck took him out midway through the fourth quarter, the Rockets were up fifteen goals to the Panthers' seven. Even though Michael had played in the attack position for only part of the game, he had scored twelve of those fifteen.

The game ended ten minutes later. The Rockets won easily, with the final score 20–11. They gave a cheer for the Panthers and slapped hands with them down the line, then started to gather up their gear.

"Good game, good game," Coach Hasbrouck said to each player.

Garry was picking up his equipment bag

when someone grabbed his arm and pulled him behind the bleachers. It was Evan.

"Hey, what gives?" Garry said, snatching his arm out of Evan's grasp and rubbing it.

"Michael wants to talk to you, remember?" Evan growled as Michael stepped out from the shadows.

"Sorry about the arm, Gar," Michael said, giving Evan a disapproving look. "Man, Evan, take it easy next time, will you? I mean, really, Garry's one of our best players, and you practically tear his arm out of its socket! Apologize to him."

Evan stared daggers at Garry. "Sorry," he muttered.

"Whatever," Garry said, turning his back on him. "What do you want, anyway?" he asked Michael.

Michael spread his hands. "Look, it's like this. Last year, our lacrosse team was number one in the league."

"That's because you were the top scorer!" Evan piped in.

Michael preened. "True, I did lead the league in goals. And I plan to do that again this year. But I also want to win the division title again, and I can't do that alone. I need solid players behind me, like you. And Evan, of course."

Evan grinned, reminding Garry of the puppy again.

"Unfortunately," Michael continued, "there are some people on the team who are dragging the rest of us down. If the league allowed players to be cut, I know of one person who'd be gone in a second." He looked meaningfully at Garry. "I think you know who I'm talking about."

"Okay, so my brother's not the greatest," Garry said. "But what do you expect me to do about it? I can't make him a good player overnight!"

"No," Michael agreed smoothly. "But you can convince him to quit."

Garry stared at him in disbelief.

"We'll be a stronger team without T.T.'s dead weight," Michael added.

Evan snickered. "'Dead weight.' I get it! 'Cause Todd's, like, fat and all!"

Michael shot a disapproving look at the other boy. Evan stopped laughing. That's when Garry heard his mother calling his name.

"I — I gotta go," he said.

Michael shot a finger gun at him. "Just think about what I said."

Garry hurried away without replying.

"There you are!" his mother said. "What were you doing?"

"Nothing. I thought I saw a dollar bill back there, but it was just a piece of trash." Garry picked up his equipment bag. "Where's Todd?"

His mother pointed toward the parking lot. "There, with Jeff. He said something about dueling cards." She looked closely at Garry. "Why? Did you need him for something? If you hurry, you can probably catch him before they take off."

Garry shook his head. "No, that's okay. I'll see him at home later, I guess."

He and his mother were heading home when suddenly she swerved into the library parking lot. "I almost forgot! I promised Dad I'd get him a new audiobook to listen to in the car. Why don't you come in with me and find something good to read while I'm looking?"

Garry sighed but opened the door and followed her into the building. While she hurried off to the adult section, he wandered into the youth area. He was browsing through some paperbacks when he heard a funny noise.

Thock! Thock! Thock!

It was coming from outside. Garry peered through a side window but didn't see anything. He listened again and realized the noise was loudest toward the back of the building. Curious, he decided to investigate.

He hurried out the front entrance and down the stone steps and started around the building. The noise was definitely coming from around the next corner. He was just about to head that way when he heard someone yell his name.

"Garry! Where *are* you?" It was his mother, standing at the top of the steps, and she sounded angry.

"Be right there, Mom!" As he waved to her, he heard muffled voices and the sound of footsteps running away. He listened closely but didn't hear anything else. Even the strange noise had stopped.

He ran around to the back of the building. There he found a small paved area just big enough for a few cars to park in. There were no cars there now, however — or anything else, for that matter. Whoever had been making the sound had left.

He had turned to join his mother when something in the grass caught his eye. He walked over and picked it up. It was his brother's stack of monster-and-magician cards. He would have recognized it anywhere.

He stood still, pondering his discovery. His mother had said that Todd was going to be trading cards with Jeff. That meant Todd had to have had the cards with him. *Since the cards are here,* Garry thought, *Todd must have been here too.* And that meant that Todd had been the one making the strange noise!

But what *was* the noise, and why had Todd abandoned his cards?

Just then his mother called his name again — and that's when Garry figured it out. Todd must have heard them calling to each other before. And when he did, he ran away, leaving his cards behind in his haste.

He hadn't been alone, though, because Garry had definitely heard two people talking. Jeff must have been there too. *And when they realized I was nearby, they took off!* The image of the two boys dropping everything in order to get away from him hit him like a wet sock in the face.

"Garry, please hurry! I have to get home!" His mother sounded impatient.

He looked down at the cards in his hands. If his mother saw them she'd wonder what he was doing with them. He didn't really feel like explaining why Todd had left them behind. So when she called again, he whipped off his sweatshirt and wrapped the cards inside it.

11

Garry planned to give Todd his cards back right away. But when he and his mother returned home, there was a message on the answering machine. It was Todd, calling to see if he could sleep at Jeff's house that night. Garry could hear Jeff laughing in the background and Todd shushing him, but laughing too. Jealousy bubbled up inside Garry, and instead of putting the cards in Todd's room, he decided to stuff them, still wrapped in his sweatshirt, into the back of his closet.

When he finally saw his brother the next

afternoon, he didn't say anything about the cards. Neither did Todd, although for a moment he looked as if he wanted to ask Garry something. Then he closed his mouth and turned away. The cards stayed hidden in Garry's closet.

"My goodness, you boys are so quiet tonight!" Mrs. Wallis observed at the dinner table later that evening.

"Just tired, I guess," Todd mumbled.

"Let me guess. You and Jeff stayed up all last night dueling those cards," she said.

Todd looked up quickly, then dropped his eyes to his plate again. "You guessed it, all right."

She shook her head and smiled. "Well, there are worse things you could be doing, I suppose."

Yeah, like treating your brother like he has the plague! Garry thought. He stole a look at

Todd, but he was pretending to be fascinated by his peas.

The brothers continued to avoid each other the next morning. Then Todd took off for Jeff's house, promising to return in time for supper.

"You know, you can have Jeff come over here sometimes too!" Mr. Wallis called out as Todd hopped onto his bike.

"That's okay, Dad," Todd replied. "We kind of like being there better."

"Well, maybe Garry would like to go with you. Where is he?" Mr. Wallis put down his paper and looked around. Garry ducked into the bathroom. By the time he came back out, Todd was long gone.

In fact, the next time Garry and Todd were anywhere near each other was at the lacrosse field on Monday afternoon. And even then they managed to steer clear of each other until the coach called the team together to outline a new drill.

"We're going to work on transitioning from defense to fast breaks today," the coach told them. "Using the whole field, we'll start play down by one goal. The defense will have control of the ball. They'll outlet a pass to a middie. That middie will carry the ball over the midfield. Running ahead of him will be the three attackers. The object will be for the offense to drive the ball as quickly as they can from one end of the field to the other. Then I want to see no less than three passes before a shot into the goal. Quick, accurate passes are key, as is running at top speed with the ball. We'll work the drill with offense only at first, then add in some defense."

He broke the team into two groups of ten, assigned each player a position, and ordered the first group out onto the field. Garry and

Michael were attackers for this group, as was Pedro. Jeff and Todd also took to the field. They were midfielders, along with Carl. Evan, Christopher, and Samuel played defense. Brandon was in goal.

Coach Hasbrouck picked up a ball, blew his whistle to get the group's attention, and threw a grounder toward the goal. Brandon hesitated for a moment, then scooped up the ball and passed it to Samuel. Samuel moved forward a few steps and threw to Carl. Carl started to jog down the field but stopped when the coach blew a sharp blast on his whistle.

"Ohh-kay," Coach Hasbrouck said, trotting onto the field. "Maybe I wasn't clear. We're working on *fast breaks* here." He reached up and plucked the ball out of Carl's pocket. "Fast means running, folks!"

Michael raised his hand. "Uh, coach, why

can't we start off with the defense team against us? I always play better when the situation is more, you know, competitive."

The coach nodded. "The defense will come in soon enough. First, I want you to practice moving the ball up the field. Tell you what, though" — he fished around in his pocket and pulled out a stopwatch — "if you really want to make it interesting, I'll time you. Ready? Set?" He threw the ball toward the goal. "Go!"

This time, Brandon didn't hesitate. He scooped up the ball and tossed it to Jeff. Jeff snared it and took off at a dead run. At the same time, Garry, Michael, and Pedro bolted toward the opposite goal. When Jeff crossed the midfield line, he hurled the ball to Pedro. Pedro made a beautiful over-the-shoulder catch, twisted the pocket around, and threw to Garry. Garry softened the catch and sent the ball to Michael. The throw was a little low, but Michael caught it, swung his stick up, and flung the ball toward the goal.

Clang!

Instead of swishing into the net, the hard ball ricocheted off the top of the goal, flying high into the air before landing in the grass. Pedro scooped it up and jogged back to the other end of the field. Garry and Michael followed.

"Seriously, Garry, why don't you just *roll* me the ball next time?" Michael groused.

Garry looked at him, with surprise. "Sorry," he said. "I guess my throw was a little off." *And so was yours,* he wanted to add.

Michael glanced at him, then grunted. "Yeah, well, just don't do it again."

Coach Hasbrouck started the drill again. This time Christopher started with the ball. He threw a quick pass to Todd. The ball looked as though it was heading to Todd's stick side. But then, at the last moment, it curved toward his left shoulder. Garry groaned inwardly, knowing his brother would never be able to make an off–stick side catch.

He was wrong. Todd whipped his stick in front of his face, made a perfect catch, and pivoted on one foot to face the attackers. Then his brother did something Garry had never seen him do before. Instead of moving his stick back to his right, he threw a weak side pass directly to Garry.

The ball came so quickly that Garry almost fumbled the catch. But he held on and managed a good pass to Michael. Michael lobbed it to Pedro and called for a pass back. Pedro had other ideas. He faked a throw to Michael, then hurled the ball into the goal.

Michael had been so sure Pedro was going to throw to him that he'd taken a step forward, stick outstretched. When the ball didn't come, he was caught off balance and stumbled a few feet before righting himself.

Garry knew better than to make any comment, but inside he silently applauded Pedro for his daring. He wasn't sure he'd have been brave enough to go up against Michael that way!

12

After they'd taken a few more trips down the field, Coach Hasbrouck called for Garry's squad to clear off so that the other group could practice the drill. When the second group was running the break smoothly, the coach put away his stopwatch. He looked up at the sky, which was filling with dark, ominous-looking clouds. "Hmm, I think we'd better move this drill along. Group two, switch to defense. Group one, back onto the field. Let's see how you do against some competition."

The two teams battled each other for the

rest of practice. By the time Coach Hasbrouck signaled for them to stop, the players were winded but feeling much more confident about working the fast break during a game situation.

The coach called them together. "As you know, we have our first game the day after tomorrow. We'll be playing against the Bulldogs. From what I hear, their bark is worse than their bite" — the team laughed — "so I don't anticipate that we'll have any problems defeating them. Still, come back here tomorrow prepared to work hard."

As Garry collected his belongings, the storm clouds opened up, sending down a drenching rain. He hurried to the parking lot, where his mother was waiting. To his surprise, Todd followed.

"What, you're not going to Jeff's again today?" he muttered as he slid into the backseat next to his brother.

"I was. But since we couldn't, um . . ." Todd's voice trailed away.

"Couldn't what?" Garry's mother asked.

"Do what we'd planned to do," Todd finished lamely, "we decided just to go home."

Garry thought about the cards, still balled up in his sweatshirt in his closet. He would have bet money that what Jeff and Todd had "planned to do" was trade cards and duel. He knew he should return the cards to their rightful owner, but for some reason he just couldn't bring himself to do it.

The next morning the sun shone brightly and the air was full of warmth. Garry looked forward to the walk to school. He decided to wait for Todd, but when he asked his brother if he was ready to go, Todd shook his head.

"I forgot something upstairs," he said. "You go on ahead."

Garry was sure his brother was pretending

he'd forgotten something just so he wouldn't have to walk with him. *Well, if that's the way he wants it, fine,* he thought. He slammed the door behind him and hurried away.

He had just crested the first hill when an acorn struck him on top of the head. He looked up right as Evan swung down from the tree above him.

"Do you live in that tree?" he asked Evan, rubbing his head. "Or do you just climb it because you're nuts about squirrels?" *Or just plain nuts,* he added silently.

"Michael wants to know if you took care of that little problem we were talking about the other day," Evan said.

Garry shifted his backpack from one shoulder to the other. "You mean, have I asked my brother to quit the team? No."

Evan stepped toward him and jabbed him in the chest. "Well, you better get on it! The first game is only two days away, and Michael does not want T.T. on the same field as him."

Suddenly Garry decided he'd had enough of Evan, and of Michael too. "Yeah, okay, fine. I'm going to make Todd quit. That's right." His voice was laced with sarcasm, which he was sure Evan wasn't smart enough to pick up on. In fact, he wasn't even sure Evan was listening to him. He seemed more interested in something behind Garry.

Whatever, Garry thought. He pushed past Evan, neither wondering nor caring if the other boy was following him or not.

At practice that afternoon Garry performed drills like a robot — moving however the play demanded but not getting any excitement or pleasure out of the game.

Maybe I'm the one who should quit, he thought at one point.

The only good part about the practice was the fact that Evan and Michael left him alone. Jeff and Todd didn't come near him either, although Garry thought Jeff seemed puzzled that he wasn't hanging out with Evan and Michael.

Todd disappeared with Jeff again after practice, and Garry headed home with his mother. Garry's mind was so far away that she had to ask him twice to add the clothes he was wearing to the dirty ones already in the washing machine.

"I did your brother's stuff earlier," she said, "and with any luck I'll be done with yours before midnight!"

Inside the bathroom, Garry stripped down; then he hurried back to his room to put on a clean set of sweats. He opened the drawer that usually held his sweatshirt collection, but it was empty. Then he remembered the sweatshirt in the back of his closet. He opened the closet door and felt around for it. His hands brushed past shoes, an old soccer ball, and something furry he couldn't identify, but no sweatshirt. He turned on the light, pushed his hanging clothes out of the way, and looked into the corner where he knew he'd thrown the sweatshirt. It wasn't there.

Then it hit him. *Todd,* he thought.

That morning, Todd had said to go on ahead without him because he'd forgotten something upstairs. *I bet he wanted me out of the house so he could search my room for his precious monster-and-magician cards!*

Well, he'd found them. Then he'd taken the sweatshirt as his way of letting Garry know he'd found them.

Garry slumped onto his bed and put his head into his hands. *Now what?* he thought. The ball was definitely on his side of the field, but he didn't know what to do with it.

13

Garry waited all through dinner that night for his brother to say something about the cards, the sweatshirt, or both. But the only thing Todd talked about was the game scheduled for the next day.

"You'll be there, right, Mom?" he asked.

"Wouldn't miss it!" she replied. She reached across the table to ruffle Todd's hair. Then she stopped and peered closely at her older son.

"What?" Todd said, leaning back from her gaze.

"You look different, somehow," she answered, still staring.

Todd flushed, a pleased smile spreading over his face. "Maybe," he said shyly, "it's because I've lost a little weight. Four pounds, actually."

Now Garry stared at his brother too. It was the first time he'd really looked at him for days, and he realized that their mother was right. Todd did look different.

Mrs. Wallis's eyes widened. "Four pounds! My goodness! All because of lacrosse?"

Todd shrugged. "That's a big part of it, I guess. Plus I'm trying not to eat junky snacks so much. Coach Hasbrouck has been helping me with that. Seems he used to have a weight problem too."

Garry tried to imagine the coach as a fat man and found he couldn't. "Wow, um, keep up the good work, Todd," he finally said.

Todd gave him a cool look. "Oh, I will," he said. "After all," he added, his voice suddenly full of meaning, "no matter what *some* people might want, I don't plan on *quitting lacrosse.*"

Garry choked on his potatoes.

"Well, I hope not," Mr. Wallis said as he thumped Garry on the back, "since it's done such a world of good for you."

Todd smiled at his parents, picked up his fork, and continued eating. Garry, on the other hand, couldn't swallow another bite.

That night he lay in bed, unable to sleep because his mind was whirling. Somehow, Todd had found out that Garry was supposed to force him to quit. But how? And how could he explain that he'd refused? His brother would just think he was lying. After all, he'd practically stolen his cards, so what was to stop him from lying too?

❄   ❄   ❄

The next morning, Todd was gone by the time Garry got downstairs. In fact, he didn't see him all day. That suited him just fine. He still hadn't figured out what, if anything, he was going to say to his brother.

When the final school bell rang, Garry hurried to the gym locker room to get ready for the game. Many of his teammates were already there, including Todd and Jeff. Garry was reaching into his locker to get his gear when he heard his brother give a sharp cry of horror. Garry peered around his locker door.

Todd was staring at his lacrosse stick, his face filled with dismay. At first Garry couldn't see what was wrong. Then Todd reached into the pocket — but instead of stopping at the mesh, his hand passed right through. Someone had slashed the netting to ribbons!

The realization had scarcely crossed Garry's

mind when Todd came charging toward him, looking angrier than Garry had ever seen him in his life.

"You did this, didn't you?" his brother yelled.

Garry recoiled in shock. "What? No, I didn't!" he protested.

"Yeah, right, like I'd believe anything you'd say!" Todd spat. "I heard you yesterday morning."

"What are you talking about?"

Todd folded his arms across his chest. "Don't play innocent with me, Garry! I heard you talking with Evan. I believe your exact words were 'I'm going to make Todd quit.'" He jerked a thumb at his lacrosse stick. "Well, it's going to take more than a stupid act of vandalism to get me off the team!"

Jeff put an arm around Todd's shoulders. "Come on, Todd," he said. "I've got a spare stick. You can use it until you get this one fixed."

Todd started to turn away, but then he stopped. "Oh, and you better give me my cards back when we get home. I know you have them!" Then he stormed off, with Jeff at his heels.

14

Garry stood stock-still, trying to process what had just happened. His own brother thought he was a liar, a thief, and a vandal! And the worst part was, even though Garry knew Todd was mistaken, he could see why he thought those things. What he couldn't see was how he was going to convince his brother that he was wrong.

Unfortunately, he didn't have time to work it out now. More players had filled the locker room to prepare for the game. If he didn't hurry, he'd be late. He quickly put on his pads, tugged his jersey over them, grabbed his helmet and stick, and headed out to the field.

He was halfway there when he realized he'd forgotten his mouth guard. With a groan, he reversed direction and went back to the locker room. As he stepped inside, he heard whispers. He recognized the voices immediately: Evan and Michael. He froze in his tracks, listening.

"I can't believe you did it! Totally awesome! I mean, that really took guts!" It was Evan, praising Michael for something yet again.

Michael gave a low chuckle. "No kidding. But you know me," he said, filling his voice with mock seriousness. "I'd do anything for the team!"

"And the best part is," Evan gloated, "he thinks Garry was the one who did it! His own brother! When really it was you who cut the mesh!"

"Yep," Michael replied. "Thanks to these here scissors!"

Garry heard the soft *snick* of scissors being opened and closed. Mouth guard forgotten, he slowly backed away, easing the door shut so that it wouldn't make a sound.

Michael was the one who ruined Todd's stick! I've got to tell Todd — and the coach! he thought frantically as he rushed back to the field.

But when he got to the field he found his mother standing with Todd. She was trying to get him to take a sweatshirt from her.

"Mom, I'm not cold," Todd said, shoving the shirt back at her.

"Just in case," she insisted.

Todd gave up. "Fine! I'll use it as a cushion." He snapped the sweatshirt open, then stared at it with a frown. "This isn't even mine, Mom."

Mrs. Wallis looked puzzled. "Isn't it? Then

what were your cards doing wrapped up inside it?"

Now it was Todd's turn to look confused. "My cards were wrapped up in this?"

Mrs. Wallis tapped her finger against her chin. "Yes, but come to think of it, I found that at the back of Garry's closet on laundry day. Guess it's his." She took the sweatshirt from Todd and handed it to Garry. "Here you go, honey. Well, good game, you two!"

"Hold on," Todd cried. "Mom, do *you* have my cards?"

She nodded apologetically. "Oh, dear, I forgot to give them back to you, didn't I? They must still be in the closet in the bathroom, above the washer. Sorry, sweetie." She gave Todd a peck on the cheek, then hurried to the bleachers.

Garry and Todd stared at each other. Finally, Garry broke the silence.

"I did have your cards," he confessed. "But

I thought you'd searched my room and found them."

"I figured you had them," Todd admitted. "Why didn't you give them back?"

Garry reddened. "I was mad at you. I know you ran away from me that day at the library."

Now it was Todd's turn to look uncomfortable. "I'm sorry about that. I just didn't want you to catch me playing . . ." His voice trailed off.

"Catch you playing what? With your cards? I've seen you play with those lots of times!"

"Not cards." Jeff joined them. "Todd, why don't you just tell him what we were doing?"

Todd sighed. "Wall ball," he finally said.

"Come again?"

"Wall ball," Todd repeated. "I was trying to get better at lacrosse by playing wall ball."

When Garry still didn't look as if he understood, Jeff explained. "Wall ball is a way to practice throwing and catching by your-self. You find a big wall, throw the ball against it, and catch it. There are different drills you can do, but basically it's throw and catch."

Garry remembered the sound he'd heard. "Then that weird noise was the ball hitting the wall," he said. "Well, why didn't you want me to know about you playing wall ball?"

"It was my idea, actually," Jeff said. "Remember that first day at practice? You seemed a little, I don't know, embarrassed by Todd." Garry hung his head. "And since it was obvious that Todd didn't know much about lacrosse" — here Todd hung *his* head — "I decided to see if I could help out. I borrowed a book of lacrosse drills from my dad and asked Todd if he'd like to get in some extra practice time with me."

"So that's what you've been doing with

Jeff all those afternoons?" Garry asked his brother.

Todd nodded. "I probably should have asked you to come too, but I don't know. I guess I wanted to surprise you or something."

Garry thought about how much better Todd had been playing lately and smiled. "You sure did surprise me. I mean, you really have improved, you know!"

Todd grinned. "Thanks, bro." Then his face darkened. "So does this mean you don't want me to quit the team anymore?"

Garry held up his hands. "Todd, I never wanted you to quit." He explained the true meaning behind what he'd said to Evan that morning. "And there's something else you should know," he added, lowering his voice. "Michael was the one who ruined your stick." In hushed tones, he told them what he'd learned in the locker room.

"We've got to tell my dad!" Jeff said when Garry had finished.

Garry had been thinking the same thing, but now he shook his head. "Michael will just deny it, and Evan will probably come to his defense, as usual."

"We can't just let him get away with it!" Jeff protested.

"We won't," Todd said, smiling a slow smile. "I have an idea, something we can do that will hit Michael right where it'll hurt him the most!" He whispered his plan to the other two boys.

Jeff grinned. "It's brilliant!" he said. "But it won't be easy. It'll be like playing the whole game a man short. And we'll have to get some of the other Rockets in on it."

"I know Pedro would be up for it," Garry said. "And I'd bet Conor would be too."

"Christopher can't stand Michael," Todd

assured them. "But stay away from Samuel and Eric. They're as much in love with him as Evan is."

"Come on," Jeff said, "if we're going to do this, we have to do it now. The game's gonna start soon."

Garry ran to the locker room to retrieve his mouth guard, then helped Todd and Jeff tell their plan to others on the team. Fifteen minutes later, more than half of their teammates had agreed to join in.

"You know, it's about time we showed Michael what teamwork is really about," Pedro said as he ran onto the field alongside Garry. Garry gave him a thumbs-up and took his position in the wings to await the face-off.

As usual, Michael was in the center for the face-off. Before the referee came onto the field, he gave Garry and Pedro his usual signals to indicate they were to pass him the ball so he could score.

"Not this time, bucko," Garry said softly. Then the game began.

Michael clamped and raked the ball clear of the circle. The ref signaled that the Rockets had possession. Garry charged forward and scooped up the ball. Michael was halfway to the Bulldogs goal and signaling for a pass.

Garry glanced at him, then hurled the ball to Pedro, who, knowing a pass was coming his way, had streaked to the center. As Pedro caught the ball on the fly, Garry rushed down the sideline. Pedro flung him the ball and ran toward the goal.

Garry had hoped to get Pedro a quick return pass, but his way was blocked by two burly Bulldogs. He heard Jeff call to him at the same time that Michael screamed for a pass. Garry stopped short, pivoted, and threw the ball — to Jeff.

Jeff dodged around a Bulldog, did a perfect inside-and-out feint, and fired the ball at the Bulldogs goal. *Swish!* Score!

"Beautiful!" Garry cried, pumping his fist in the air. Pedro high-fived Jeff on the way back to their starting positions. Michael looked as if he couldn't believe what had just happened.

He had the same look three minutes later, when Jeff, Garry, Pedro, and Conor worked the ball around the field until Conor was able to take a shot. The ball hit the net, billowing it out backward, and another point was added to the Rockets side of the scoreboard. The Rockets cheered loudly.

The Bulldogs, meanwhile, seemed confused that the Rockets weren't passing to Michael.

"I thought the coach told us that number twenty-seven was the one to watch," Garry overheard one Bulldog say to another. "That guy's not doing anything!"

Garry grinned. That was Michael they were talking about!

Coach Hasbrouck took Michael, Garry, and Pedro out of the game at the end of the first quarter. "But, Coach," Garry heard Michael complain, "I haven't scored."

"And yet we're still winning five to one," the coach answered, "so we must be doing something right."

Michael had no answer for that. He sat down, frowning. Garry and Pedro exchanged delighted looks, then turned their attention back to the game.

Evan was now on the front line with Todd and Conor. Jeff was still in the game. He scooped up the ball after Conor raked it free in the face-off. With a quick flick, he sent it to

Todd. It was a hard throw and Todd fumbled the ball. As it dropped to the ground, Michael snorted with disgust.

"What a loser," the older boy said.

Garry stood up, walked over to where Michael was sitting, and stared down at him.

"Hey, Wallis, clear off. You're in my way!" Michael said.

"I'm going to say this one time, Donofrio," Garry said, his voice so low and menacing that Michael looked up at him with surprise. "Stop knocking my brother. He's here to stay and he's here to play."

"And if I don't?" Michael replied, narrowing his eyes.

"Then you can kiss any chance of being the league top scorer good-bye."

Michael's jaw dropped. "Did you hear that?" he said to Christopher, who was sitting next to him. "Can you believe what he just said to me?"

Christopher looked from Michael to Garry and back. "Yeah," he replied. "Wish I'd said it. Now pipe down so I can pay attention to the game."

Garry grinned the whole way back to his seat. He was still smiling when he went back into the game halfway through the second quarter — and when he scored the first of his four goals that game. The Rockets took the win easily, beating the Bulldogs 17–10. Michael had scored only two goals.

After the game, Coach Hasbrouck called the team together. "I'm proud of you boys," he said. "You did a great job working that ball around today. Even better, you made good use of every player on the field."

He put his hands in his pockets and looked up at the sky. "You know, my objective for this team is to make each of you better players by the end of the season. And the only way for me to do that is to make sure you get plenty of experience. That's why I make sure everyone on this team gets equal playing time."

He turned his gaze back to the team. "I know some of you don't like sitting on the bench. You think your place is on the field, scoring goals," — he glanced at Michael — "and that the measure of a good team is how many goals you score against the other side."

He spread his hands. "But in my opinion, the strongest teams are those made up of players who work together. Like you all did today." He grinned. "Okay, enough speeches for one day. Gather your stuff and head on home!"

Garry picked up his stick and his equipment bag.

"Coach Hasbrouck is such a turkey," he heard Evan whisper to Michael.

"No kidding," Michael replied, his disgust plain. "Get my gear, will you?"

"Sure thing, bro!"

Garry shook his head. Michael and Evan, he realized, would never change. But that was okay. *After all,* he thought, watching his brother horse around with Jeff, *there are plenty of other people I'd rather hang out with!*

Matt Christopher®

Sports Bio Bookshelf

Kobe Bryant

Terrell Davis

John Elway

Julie Foudy

Jeff Gordon

Wayne Gretzky

Ken Griffey Jr.

Mia Hamm

Tony Hawk

Grant Hill

Derek Jeter

Randy Johnson

Michael Jordan

Lisa Leslie

Tara Lipinski

Mark McGwire

Greg Maddux

Hakeem Olajuwon

Alex Rodriguez

Briana Scurry

Sammy Sosa

Tiger Woods

Steve Young

The #1 Sports Series for Kids

Read them all!

All available in paperback from Little, Brown and Company